Kunu's Basket

A STORY FROM INDIAN ISLAND

Lee DeCora Francis

Illustrated by Susan Drucker

TILBURY HOUSE PUBLISHERS · THOMASTON, MAINE

"I can't do it. It's too hard. I just can't make baskets," Kunu muttered, turning away from the tangle of ash strips.

"Would you like some help?" asked his dad.

"No, thanks. I want to do it myself." He looked one more time at the pile of ash strips. "I'm going outside for a while before I try again."

Muhmum watched from his porch next door as the boy plunked down on a log

and began tapping the ash strips together—slowly.

"What's wrong, Grandson? Why the sad face?"

"Well, I just want to make baskets like you and my dad. I keep trying, but I can't do it."

Muhmum smiled. All the men in the family made baskets. It was something that they were known for on the island. He was glad to see Kunu with the ash strips in his hands.

"*Che-gwe, gwos.* Come here, my son. I could use help pounding this ash."

Muhmum pointed to a spot on the log and asked Kunu to make a mark there.

"That's good. Now I'll know exactly where to pound."

Kunu watched. *Doonk, doonk, doonk.* "Can I do that, too?"

"Sure. Hold the axe like this and pound right where you marked it."

Kunu swung and missed the spot—twice. He looked at his grandfather.

"You just need practice. Try again."

This time Kunu hit the mark with an echoing *doonk*.

"Look, *gwos*. These strips are already pounded. You can help me pull them."

Kunu pulled the strips back carefully.

"Great work, *gwos*."

After a short rest, Muhmum asked Kunu to go with him to the workshop. "I have
to start a few new basket bottoms. Do you think you could help me with them?"

"Sure." Kunu nodded and followed his grandfather.

Kunu sat at the table and waited while Muhmum gathered the supplies they would need.

Muhmum showed Kunu the way to make the bottom for the basket. "It's important to have a strong base. You want it just right or your whole basket will be weak."

But when Kunu tried to set up the ash strips, they kept slipping out of place. Muhmum made it look so easy.

"This isn't working."

Muhmum looked up from his own work and pointed to something in the corner of the room. "See that basket over there by the shelves? That is my first pack basket. I made it when I was about your age. Can you guess how many tries it took for me to get the bottom just right?"

Kunu shook his head.

"Seven tries! Take your time, *gwos*, and try again."

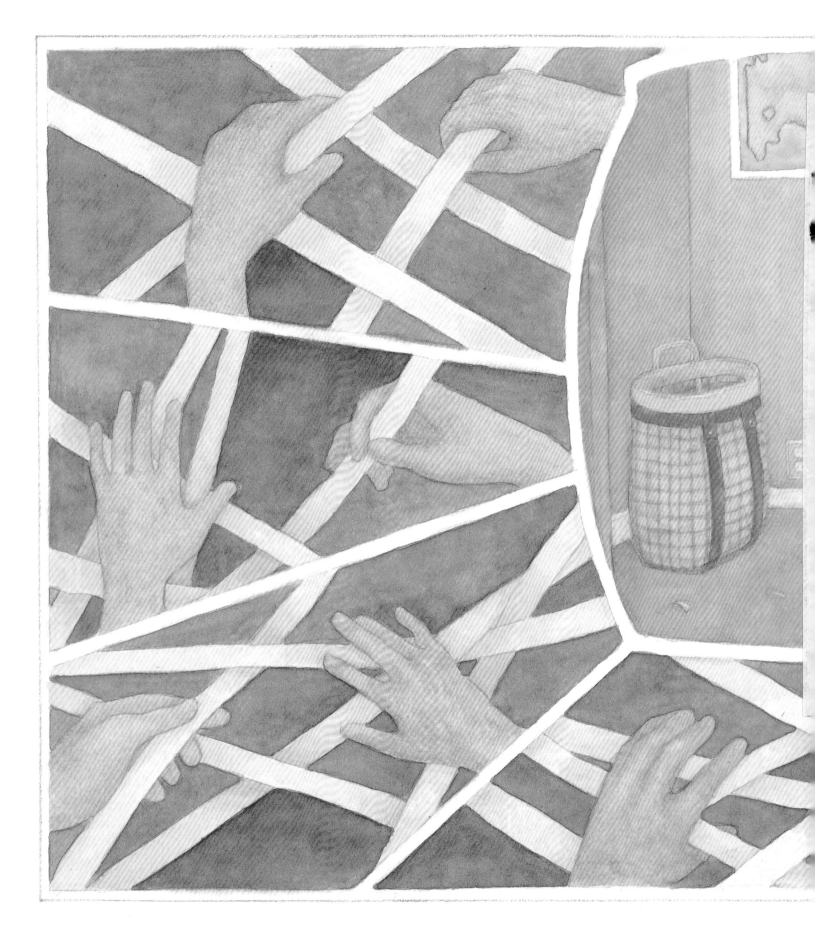

"There. That looks good," said Muhmum.

"I did it," Kunu whispered.

Next, Muhmum showed how to set the block of wood on the base.

"This is the block that will help your basket take on the right shape," he explained.

"I used this one to make my first basket."

Kunu looked over at the little basket in the corner and smiled.

"That's enough for now," his grandfather said. "Let's have lunch. We can start weaving tomorrow."

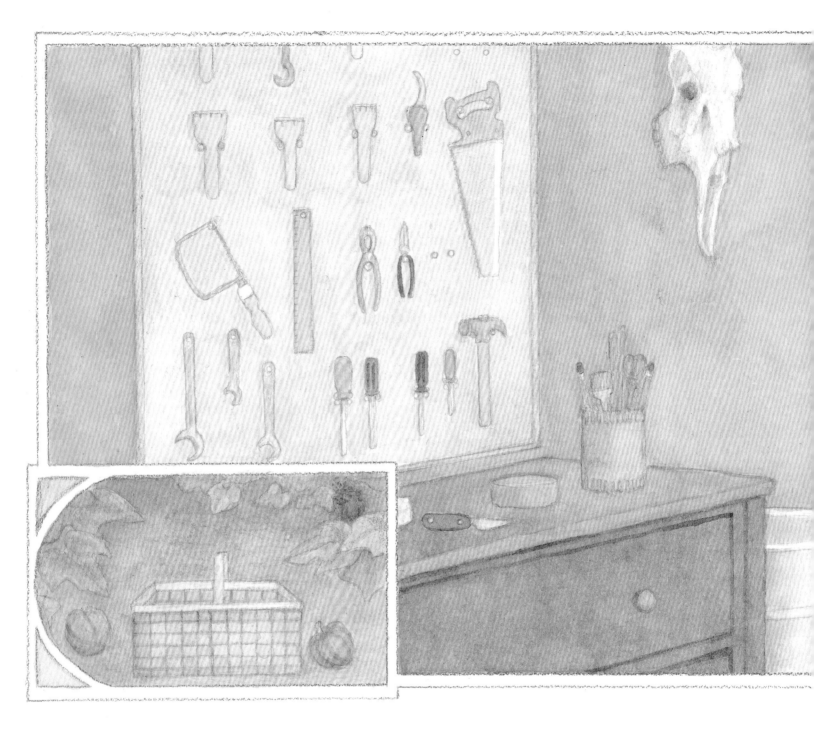

The next day Muhmum showed Kunu how to slip ash strips back and forth among the upright strips called standards. "Take your time, *gwos*. You want it just right."

Kunu was very excited. He started to weave as fast as he could. But then, when he stood back to look at his work, he got very quiet. "This doesn't look right."

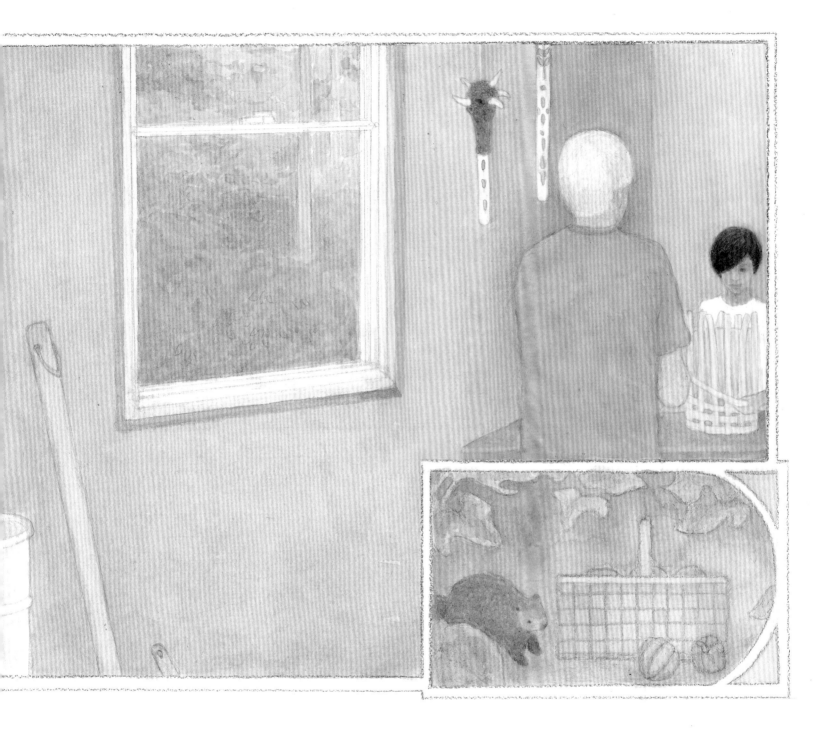

Muhmum said nothing, but pointed at the pack basket in the corner.

"Seven tries?" asked Kunu.

"Seven tries," Muhmum answered with a wink.

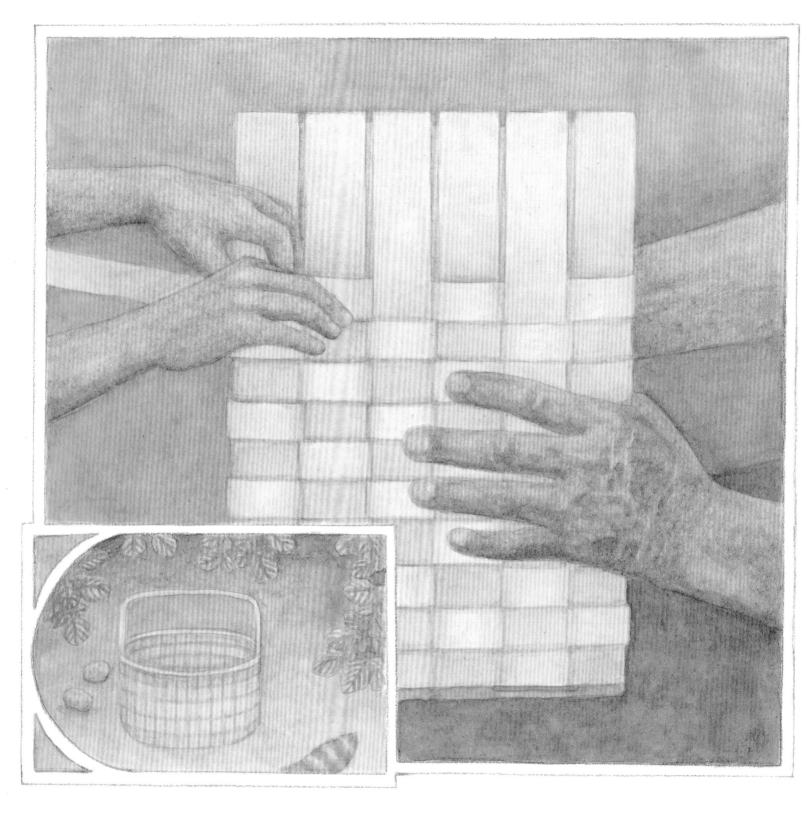

Kunu took a deep breath and started over, more slowly this time. With each woven strip, he could feel his basket getting stronger.

"Muhmum, I think this might be strong enough to hold all of my things!"

"You might be right," his grandfather replied.

When Kunu was almost done with the weaving, his grandfather helped him take the basket off the block.

"Finishing off the rim can be pretty hard," Muhmum said. "Do you want to do that part together?"

Kunu thought for a few moments. He pointed to the pack basket in the corner and asked, "Did anyone help you with the rim on your basket?"

"Yes, my grandfather," replied Muhmum.

Kunu kept listening.

"Basket making is something that the sons in our family have learned from our fathers and grandfathers going back a long, long way. My grandfather taught me how to do the rim just as I'll show you."

"*Gwos*, now you are done. All you need are the straps—and I think I know where you can get some."

Muhmum went over to his own pack basket in the corner and removed the straps. He put them on Kunu's new basket.

"Try it on, *gwos*. Let's see how you look."

"Wow!" said Kunu, as he settled the straps on his shoulders and felt the basket strong against his back. Kunu hugged his grandfather. "Thank you, Muhmum."

"Thank you, Grandson. Run home now and show your dad."

Muhmum watched the new pack bounce on his grandson's back as he skipped

through the yard. He smiled as he heard Kunu shout, "I did it, Dad! I really did it.

I made a basket!"

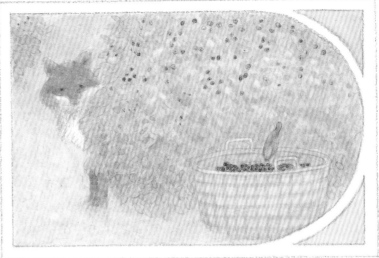

Basket making is an important tradition in the Penobscot Indian Nation. It is an art my people have practiced for generations upon generations. Long ago, our baskets were used in countless daily tasks, such as gathering berries, picking fiddleheads (the edible ferns of spring, as pictured in this book), transporting supplies, and even carrying children.

During my grandparents' and great-grandparents' time, when the Penobscot people were living through severe economic hardships, many made baskets to help support their families financially. Skilled basket makers worked long hours, often in groups, to produce beautiful baskets that they hoped would fetch a fair price.

 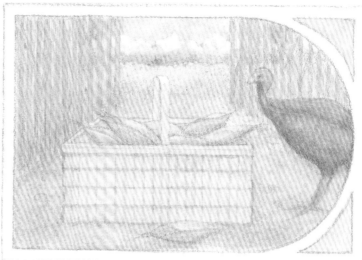

A lot of work goes into a single basket. One has to harvest trees, pound them, split them, and prepare the strips in order to begin the weaving process. Many basket makers received very little compensation for their time, but it was still necessary to sell their wares in order to provide for their families. Some traveled along the coast of Maine during the summer, often visiting the same locations year after year to sell baskets to tourists. In the fall they returned home to begin making baskets for the next season.

Today, skilled basket makers showcase their work at museums and events in Maine and across the country. This knowledge has given many of my people opportunities to support their families, but more importantly, it provides a pathway for passing our traditions from one generation to another. This is why *Kunu's Basket* is a story that needed to be told.

When I started writing *Kunu's Basket*, I wanted to pay tribute to this art that supported so many people, including my own family. I also wanted to share a glimpse of the Penobscot people with others. But what I wanted most was to capture the bonds that often exist between our youth and elders. I wanted to share relationships that I have known and experienced as a way to honor people who have been special in my life. My hope is that while you read this story, it will remind you of someone special in yours.

T'gok

Sandy Beach

Lover's Leap

Fort Dawson

Oak Hill

Beaver Flowage

Breezy Hill

Elizabeth's Shore

Second Ledge

First Ledge

Head of Island

Joe Pease

Hollywood

Blueberry Barrens

Nick Andrew's Shore

The Pond

The Landing

ABOUT THE AUTHOR AND ILLUSTRATOR

Lee DeCora Francis (Penobscot/HoChunk) comes from both the Penobscot Indian Nation in Maine and the Winnebago Tribe of Nebraska. She is a teacher at the tribal elementary school located at the Penobscot Nation. She lives on Indian Island in Maine with her husband, two beautiful sons, and their cat.

Susan Drucker has loved drawing and painting since she was a child. An illustrator and artist, she lives with her husband in Bowdoinham, Maine, and has two grown children. She is thankful to have had the opportunity to learn about the Penobscot Indians while working on this book.

For suggestions for using this book in the classroom, please visit www.tilburyhouse.com.

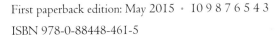

TILBURY HOUSE PUBLISHERS

12 Starr Street

Thomaston, Maine 04861

800–582–1899 · www.tilburyhouse.com

First paperback edition: May 2015 · 10 9 8 7 6 5 4 3

ISBN 978-0-88448-461-5

For Ben, my Kunu —Lee Francis

To Hank, with love —Susan Drucker

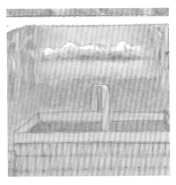

Library of Congress Cataloging-in-Publication Data

Francis, Lee DeCora, 1972-

  Kunu's basket / Lee DeCora Francis ; illustrated by Susan Drucker. — 1st hardcover ed.

    p. cm.

  Summary: Feeling frustrated when his first attempt to make a basket fails, a
Penobscot Indian boy receives help and encouragement from his grandfather.

  ISBN 978-0-88448-330-4 (hardcover : alk. paper)

[1. Basket making—Fiction. 2. Perserverance (Ethics)—Fiction. 3. Grandfathers—
Fiction. 4. Penobscot Indians—Fiction. 5. Indians of North America—Maine—
Fiction. 6. Maine—Fiction.] I. Drucker, Susan, 1959- ill. II. Title.

  PZ7.F84675Ku 2012

  [E]—dc23

                    2011026590

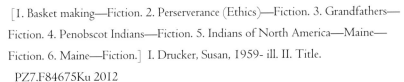

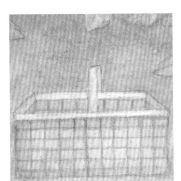

Designed by Geraldine Millham, Westport, Massachusetts

Printed by United Graphics, Mattoon, IL 61938

(April 2016) Batch 66915-0